Scholastic Publications Ltd.,
10 Earlham Street, London WC2H 9RX, UK

Scholastic Inc.,
730 Broadway, New York, NY 10003, USA

Scholastic Tab Publications Ltd.,
123 Newkirk Road, Richmond Hill,
Ontario L4C 3G5, Canada

Ashton Scholastic Pty. Ltd.,
P O Box 579, Gosford, New South Wales,
Australia

Ashton Scholastic Ltd.,
165 Marua Road, Panmure, Auckland 6,
New Zealand

First published by Scholastic Publications Limited, 1988
Text copyright © John Cunliffe, 1988
Illustrations copyright © Scholastic Publications Limited and
Woodland Animations Limited, 1988
Reprinted 1988

ISBN 0 590 70960 7

Made and printed in Hong Kong
Typeset in Times Roman by AKM Associates (UK) Ltd,
Ajmal House, Hayes Road, Southall, London

Postman Pat
Goes Sailing

Story by **John Cunliffe** Pictures by **Joan Hickson**
From the original Television designs by **Ivor Wood**

Hippo Books
in association with André Deutsch

"Letters for the island?" said Pat. "I thought there was nobody living there."

"There *was* nobody living there," said Mrs Goggins. "But there is now. I've always said it's a shame, that house standing empty, and such a lovely house, too."

"I don't think I'd like to live in the middle of a lake," said Pat, "even if it is lovely. There'll be nobody to talk to when you're digging the garden. When did they move in?"

"Yesterday," said Mrs Goggins. "It's a wonder you didn't see them."

"I was busy chasing bees," said Pat.

5

"They sent a big boat up from Brockwood to get their furniture across. There was a right to do."

"Mr and Mrs Shackleton," said Pat, looking at the envelopes. "I wonder if they get many letters?"

"You'll have to practise your rowing," said Mrs Goggins.

"I don't think Jess is going to like having a boat trip every day," said Pat.

Pat went on his way. When he came to
the lake, he walked out onto the little
jetty where the boats tie up. There was a
strong wind blowing. Pat held onto his
hat, and he held onto Jess, too. Tied up
to a ring was a small rowing-boat,
rocking up and down in the waves made
by the wind.

"Seems a bit rough today," said Pat.
"But the post must get through. I'm sure
Ted won't mind if I borrow his boat. So
. . . here we go, Jess."

The boat seemed very small. The waves seemed to be getting bigger. When Pat stepped in to the boat, the side he stood on dipped down and almost tipped them in to the water.

"Ooops!" said Pat, "Oh! Help! Ouch!"
He had tripped over an oar, and
tumbled in to the bottom of the boat. He
found quite a lot of cold water there.
Then he scrambled on to the seat, and
Jess curled up in the driest place he could
find, in the very middle of the boat. Now
that Pat was sitting in the middle of the
seat, the boat balanced nicely. But then

he said, "Oh, no!" because he had to stand up again to untie the boat. This was not easy. The boat wobbled and shook, and Jess thought he would have to swim for it at any moment. He wished he had stayed by Mrs Goggins' warm fire.

"We could do with a pair of life-jackets," said Pat.

Pat managed to get the rope off, and sat
down again with a bump. Then he had to
get the oars into place, and that meant
more splashing.

11

At last they were ready to go.
Pat began to pull on the oars, heading
out across the lake. It was hard work.
He rowed hard for quite a time.
Then he stopped to look round, to see
how far away the island was now.

"Oh dear, we haven't gone far," said
Pat.

There was a long stretch of choppy

water between Pat and the island, and the jetty still seemed quite near.

"The trouble with rowing," said Pat, "is that you can't see where you're going."

Jess thought there were many more things *he* didn't like about rowing; the wave that had just splashed him was one of them.

The harder Pat rowed, the harder the wind pushed them back to the jetty. When Pat stopped to rest or look round, the wind didn't rest, it just went on pushing.

"It'll be easier coming back," said Pat, "with the wind behind us."

After ten minutes of hard rowing they were not even half way to the island.

Then Pat heard a shout coming from behind him. He was so surprised that he almost fell out of the boat! It was Ted Glen. He was out in his sailing boat. Ted went whizzing past at speed.

"My goodness," said Pat, "that's better than rowing."

Ted went past so fast that Pat only heard part of what he was shouting. It sounded like, "Hi, Pat! Where . . . you . . . trying . . . ? I'll just . . hang on!"

Ted couldn't stop, because the wind that
was pushing Pat back was filling Ted's
sails and pushing him along so fast that
Ted was soon far away across the lake,
and going round behind the island.

"Well, that was a short visit," said Pat.

And all this time Pat was being blown back to the jetty. Then Ted appeared again, round the island, and seemed to be zig-zagging back towards Pat and Jess. He had rolled up some of his sails, so he was going more slowly now.

"Go back to the jetty!" Ted shouted. "I'll fetch you a life-jacket."

Pat didn't need telling twice. He was glad to turn round and row with the help of the wind. He was soon at the jetty. Ted sailed up to Pat.

"Where are you trying to get to?" he said.

"I've got some letters for the island," said Pat.

"You'll never row there in this wind," said Ted. "You'd best come in my boat. I'll have you there in no time at all."

Pat tied up the rowing boat, and climbed into Ted's boat with Jess tucked into his jacket.

Pat had never been in a sailing boat before, and Ted hadn't done any sailing for over a year, as he had been busy mending and painting the boat. Pat sat down in the middle of the boat, as far away from the water as he could get.

"Now, then," said Ted, "it's no good sitting there. You'll have to sit out."

"Sit out?" said Pat. "Whatever do you mean? How can you sit *out* of a boat? I thought we were coming *in* it!"

"It's not the same in a sailing boat,"
said Ted. "You see, you have to balance
it. You sit on the side. Then, when it tips
over, you lean out the other side to
balance it. It'll sink if you don't."

"But I'll fall in the water if I lean out,"
said Pat.

"No, you won't," said Ted. "Just tuck
your feet into these straps. They'll hold
you. You'll soon get the hang of it."

"But . . ." said Pat.

"Hold tight!" said Ted. "We're off!"

They were. Ted had put up the sails, and loosened the rope. The wind filled the sails, and they skimmed across the water. In a minute, the jetty was far away. The boat leaned farther and farther over, as the wind pushed on the sails. Ted leaned right out of the boat, almost touching the water.

"Sit out, Pat!" he shouted. "Farther!"

Pat copied Ted. He held onto a rope
for dear life, and sat far out of the boat.
The water looked very cold. He didn't
want the boat to tip over, and it felt as if
it would do, at any moment. So Pat leaned
out much farther than he really dared.

"Can you swim?" shouted Ted.

"Not very well," said Pat, but Ted was
busy with the boat, and didn't seem to
hear.

"We're going about," shouted Ted. "Get ready . . ."

"What . . . ?" said Pat.

"Now!" shouted Ted. "*Move!*"

"Where?" said Pat. "Oh!"

"Get your head down," Ted yelled.

Suddenly, the boat swung round, so
that the wind came from the other side.
The sail came swinging across, just
missing Pat's head as he ducked down.
The boat tipped over the other way now.
Ted scrambled across to the other side of
the boat, and Pat followed him.

They leaned out to balance it again, and it whizzed across the water, bouncing through the waves, and making waves of its own. In this way, they went in zig-zag lines across the lake. The island was far behind them, now.

"Er, Ted, I wanted to get to the island with these letters. We seem to have gone a long way past it," said Pat.

"It's called *tacking*," said Ted.

"I think we've dropped a few stitches," said Pat.

"No, it's because of the wind," said Ted. "It depends on the way the wind's blowing. Ready to go about! Now . . . ! You can't sail the opposite way to the wind, so you have to go in zig-zags till you're where you want to be. Ready! We're going about!"

They went zig-zagging about the lake
in this way for some time. At times, the
island was quite near, at others they
couldn't even see it. When they were near
it, Ted said the wind wasn't right, and
they'd not be able to land this time
round.

"Lovely day for a sail," said Ted.

"Yes," said Pat, "but I've got these
letters to deliver, and I should be getting
on."

28

"Oh, we'll make it next time round," said Ted.

But they didn't.

"Let's try once more," said Ted.

They missed it again, but passed near enough to wave to Mr and Mrs Shackleton, who were standing on the island's jetty, watching them.

"You could put the letters in a bottle, and float them across," said Ted, laughing.

29

When they missed yet again, Ted said,
"It's no good. That wind's not right.
We'll have to put ashore. Tell you what,

Pat. We'll nip up to Dr Gilbertson's
place, and see if she can get her old
motorboat out. That should do the trick."

Ted landed at the jetty, and tied the boat
up safely. Pat was glad to be on land
again. He felt very odd. It felt strange to
be walking on something that didn't tip

from side to side. As he walked along the
jetty he zig-zagged as much as the boat
had done on the water.

"You've got your sea-legs, now," said
Ted.

It took Pat a long time to learn how to walk in a straight line again.

"It's a lucky thing you can drive in a straight line," said Ted, as they went on their way to Dr Gilbertson's.

The doctor was glad to see them, as Pat had a lot of letters for her, and a parcel.

"Pat, was that you I saw," said Dr Gilbertson, "out rowing on the lake? I got my binoculars out, and it looked very much like you. But I said to Peter, it can't be Pat, because he'll be busy with his letters at this time of day."

Pat told her all about his struggles to get to the island with the letters for the new people, and Ted asked about her motorboat.

"You're welcome to borrow it, if you can get it to go," said Dr Gilbertson. "I can't remember when I last had it out. Better still, I'll come with you. They're sure to need a doctor on that island, one of these days, so it'll be good practice. Oh, and I must give the Reverend a ring. He loves boats. I'm sure he'd like to come."

At the end of Dr Gilbertson's garden was the lake, and on the edge of the water was the old boathouse. What an odd house it was! There was a dry door at the garden end, for people, and there was a wet door at the lake end for the boat. There was a little jetty inside, where the boat was tied up. It was a good thing they had Ted

there. It was such a long time since the boat had been out that the engine didn't want to start. Ted asked for an old towel, then for a paperclip. He opened hatches, turned knobs, tightened up screws, and pulled hard on the hand-starter.

In the end, he had to borrow the battery from Pat's van. The engine started with a bang and a puff of blue smoke, churning up the water in the boat-house, and making the boat pull hard on its ropes.

"We're off!" said Ted. "All aboard!"

The Reverend Timms arrived just in time.

"What a wonderful chance to call on our new neighbours," he said. "I must welcome them to our little church."

Off they all went, across the lake to the island. Dr Gilbertson steered, and Ted kept an eye on the engine. The Reverend sang a stirring hymn about the sea.

37

"This is fun," said Dr Gilbertson. "I shall take up boating again."

"Remind me to get you a battery," said Ted.

"I like your boat," said Pat. "There are two good things about it. One, we can sit *in* it, instead of sitting *out* of it. Two, it goes in a straight line, instead of making these stitches that you have to do in a sailing boat."

"Tacking," said Ted. "There's nothing like sailing."

"What has sewing got to do with boats?" said Dr Gilbertson.

But they arrived at the island, so no one had time to answer her. The Shackletons were waiting on their jetty. They were very glad to see them.

"Welcome to the island," said Mr Shackleton.

"I'm afraid it's rather an invasion," said the Reverend Timms.

"Oh, not a bit of it," said Mrs Shackleton. "Come and have some tea. We've had the kettle on for ages. We thought you'd never make it. It is a bit rough today."

They had tea, and sandwiches, and cakes. They were delicious. Pat delivered his letters. The Reverend Timms put the Shackletons' names down for the choir, the pet show, and the coach trip to Blackpool. Ted spotted a clock that needed mending, and Dr Gilbertson gave them a card with her telephone number on it, "Just in case."

"I'll have to be getting on with my letters," said Pat.

"Call again," said Mrs Shackleton. "But don't worry Pat, about having to set sail with our letters every day. We'll come over and collect them from Mrs Goggins from now on."

"Thanks," said Pat. "It'll save me from getting my feet wet."

"And all that tacking," said Ted.

"I'll have to tack up the valley with these letters," said Pat.

They all said, "Cheerio! And thanks for the tea."

And off they went, in Dr Gilbertson's motorboat. Ted had a turn at steering, and Pat kept an eye on the engine. When they got back, Pat's van wouldn't start.

"Your battery's in the boat," said Ted. "Hang on, I'll pop it back for you."

Pat was soon on his way. He went along winding roads up into the hills, to the end of the valley, and down the far side of the lake. Jess curled up in his basket and went to sleep. From time to time, he shook dream-water from his whiskers.

"Never mind, Jess," said Pat. "We'll soon be sailing home, and there'll be a good tea waiting for us."